To:

_____

From:

_____

D1445088

A Few Words from the Author

It's curious how the idea of going to bed tends to grow on us as we get older. As a child, I avoided bedtime at all costs. Sleep signified an ending—the absence of play, of exploration, of fun. Life was simply too exciting and full of possibility to prioritize anything as trivial as sleep, and the more tired I grew, the more I resisted it.

But if the process of going to bed is turned into a game of sorts, it becomes much more appealing. When I wrote this story in 1983, I realized the importance of engaging in imaginative play with my children. I tried to meet them in their world. At the end of the day, they just wanted to feel that they were going to bed on their own terms. And, of course, they wanted to be reassured that sleep was only an intermission—and play would resume in the morning. I hope this book—and every other Little Critter book—will be an inspiration to create new ways to make bedtime more enjoyable for children and parents alike.

—Mercer Mayer

"Usually an idea, like the process of going to bed, will ruminate in the back of my mind for a period of time while I work on other projects. I make a quick sketch or jot down some notes, but I allow the story to form on its own in its own time. Stories are almost like independent beings that wander around out there. You have to stay out of their way, and they come in." —Mercer Mayer

Just Go to Bed book, characters, text, and images copyright © 1983, 2021 by Mercer Mayer. Little Critter, Mercer Mayer's Little Critter, and Mercer Mayer's Little Critter and Logo are registered trademarks of Orchard House Licensing Company. All rights reserved. Published in the United States by Random House Children's Books, a division of Penguin Random House LLC, 1745 Broadway, New York, NY 10019, and in Canada by Penguin Random House Canada Limited, Toronto. Originally published by Golden Books, an imprint of Random House Children's Books, New York, in 1983. Random House and the colophon are registered trademarks of Penguin Random House LLC.

Visit us on the Web!
rhcbooks.com
littlecritter.com

Educators and librarians, for a variety of teaching tools, visit us at RHTeachersLibrarians.com

ISBN 978-0-593-37623-2 (hardcover)

MANUFACTURED IN CHINA

10 9 8 7 6 5 4 3 2 1

JUST GO TO BED

BY MERCER MAYER

Random House ⌂ New York

I'm a cowboy and I round up cows.
I can lasso anything.

Dad says . . .

"It's time for the cowboy to come inside and get ready for bed."

I'm a general and I have to stop
the enemy army with my tank.

Dad says . . .

"It's time for the general to take a bath."

I'm a space cadet and I zoom to the moon.

I capture a robot with my ray gun.

Dad says . . .

"This giant robot has captured the space cadet and is going to put him in the bathtub right now."

I'm a sea monster attacking a ship.

Dad says, "It's time for the sea monster to have a snack."

I'm a zookeeper feeding my hungry animals.

Dad says . . .

"Feeding time is over. Here are the zookeeper's pajamas."

I'm Super Critter flying over the city.

I'm a train engineer being chased by bandits.

ELECT-O SUPER

Dad says, "The bandit chief has caught you, so put on your pajamas."

But I'm a race car driver and I just speed away.

Dad says, "The race is over.
Now put on these pajamas
and go to bed."

I'm a bunny hopping
around my garden.

Dad says . . .

"Just go to bed!"

"But I'm a bunny and bunnies don't sleep in a bed."

Mom says, "Shhh!"
Dad says, "Go to sleep."

Well, maybe a tired bunny could sleep in a bed . . . just this once.

Wait, there's more!

Turn the page to look at never-before-seen
sketches by Mercer Mayer, the author and
illustrator of Little Critter!

A LOOK BEHIND THE BOOK!

Like most illustrators, Mercer Mayer starts the artwork for each book with a rough sketch of every page, plus the cover. This way, he can figure out where to put the characters and leave space for the words.

I'M A BUNNY AND I HOP 'ROUND THE GARDEN PATCH

DAD SAYS "GO TO BED NOW".

Illustrators also add background details in the sketch stage. Background details help the reader figure out where the character is and what is happening.

I'LL STAY AWAKE ALL NIGHT LONG

BUT FIRST I'LL REST JUST A LITTLE

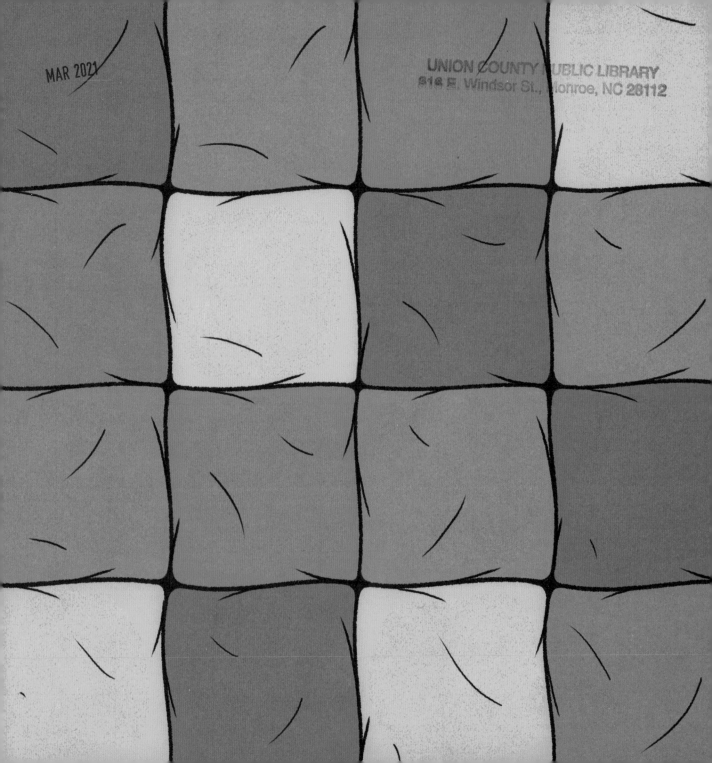